220031

D1152163

NICHOLAS ALLAN

A PIG'S BOOK OF MANNERS

RED FOX

FALKIRK COUNCIL
LIBRARY SUPPORT
FOR SCHOOLS

FALKIRK COUNCIL
LIBRARY SUPPORT
FOR SCHOOLS

To my nephews – Benjamin, Charlie, Henry and Jamie

A Red Fox Book

Published by Random House Children's Books
20 Vauxhall Bridge Road, London SW1V 2SA

A division of Random House UK Ltd
London Melbourne Sydney Auckland
Johannesburg and agencies throughout the world

Copyright © Nicholas Allan 1995

1 3 5 7 9 10 8 6 4 2

First published in Great Britain by
Hutchinson Children's Books 1995

Red Fox edition 1997

This book is sold subject to the condition that it shall not, by way of trade or otherwise, be lent, resold, hired out, or otherwise circulated without the publisher's prior consent in any form of binding or cover other than that in which it is published and without a similar condition including this condition being imposed on the subsequent purchaser.

The right of Nicholas Allan to be identified as the author and illustrator of this work has been asserted by him in accordance with the Copyright, Designs and Patents Act, 1988.

Printed in Hong Kong

RANDOM HOUSE UK Limited Reg. No. 954009

ISBN 0 09 953391 X

This is Johnny Squelchnose on his way to Lucy's party.

Here he is wishing Lucy a happy birthday.

Here he is admiring Lucy's new bike.

Here he is eating jelly without a spoon…

…and asking for cake when he hasn't finished his jelly.

Here he is after tea…

…and a little later after tea.

Here he is thanking Lucy for a lovely time.

And here's Johnny Squelchnose wondering why he's not invited to any more parties.

'You're a PIG!' said his big sister. 'A PIG! That's what *you* are.'

Now, just at that moment, someone new was moving in next door.

Claude Curlytail's phone never stopped ringing... nor did his door bell...

...and he was off to parties *every* afternoon!

...thought Johnny Squelchnose.

One day Claude felt so sorry for Johnny he invited him
to his friend Jenny's picnic.

It was funny walking along the road with a pig, but no one seemed to notice.

When they arrived Claude said, 'This is my friend Johnny.'
  'Hello,' said Jenny.
  'Grunt,' said Johnny.
  Claude gave Jenny a cake for the picnic.

'That Claude's *so* nice,' said Jenny.

…whispered Johnny Squelchnose.

Claude saw Jenny's new skateboard.
'Please, can I have a go on it – after you?' he asked.

'That Claude's *so* considerate,' said Jenny.

...said Johnny Squelchnose.

At tea there were only two pieces of cake left. Johnny took one. Claude offered the other to Roger.

'That Claude's *so* kind,' said Roger.

...spluttered Johnny Squelchnose.

After tea Claude helped clear up…while Johnny picked his nose.

'That Claude's *so* helpful,' said Jenny's dad.

...shrieked Johnny Squelchnose.

Some time after the picnic, Claude asked, 'Please, can I go to the lavatory?'... while Johnny *didn't* ask.

'That Claude's *so* polite,' said Jenny's mum.

...squealed Johnny Squelchnose.

But no one listened to Johnny Squelchnose. They all wanted to be with Claude Curlytail. Until Johnny wished *he* was Claude (even if Claude *was* a pig).

So when it was time to go and Claude said, 'Thanks for a lovely picnic',
Johnny said … 'Thanks for a lovely picnic, too', and everyone smiled.
      'Thanks for coming,' said Jenny.
      Johnny felt better already.

The next day Johnny invited Claude and his friends to tea.

Johnny set the table, handed round the chocolate cake and poured the orange juice.

'What a polite boy!' beamed Mr Squelchnose.

But afterwards they played games, and got louder
and *louder* and LOUDER.

Until Mr Squelchnose came storming in.
   'What's all this noise?' he shouted. 'You're *elephants!*
ELEPHANTS! That's what you lot are!'

Just at that moment someone new was moving in – very quietly –
next door.

FALKIRK COUNCIL
LIBRARY SUPPORT
FOR SCHOOLS